AND THE PANDORA PLOT

WRITTEN BY
IVAN COHEN

ILLUSTRATED BY
GREGG SCHIGIEL

WONDER WOMAN CREATED BY
WILLIAM MOULTON MARSTON

STONE ARCH BOOKS
a capstone imprint

Published by Stone Arch Books,
an imprint of Capstone.
1710 Roe Crest Drive
North Mankato, Minnesota 56003
www.capstonepub.com

Library of Congress Cataloging-in-Publication Data
is available on the Library of Congress website.
ISBN: 978-1-4965-8724-4 (library binding)
ISBN: 978-1-4965-9202-6 (paperback)
ISBN: 978-1-4965-8728-2 (eBook PDF)

Summary: When Giganta steals a mysterious ancient jar
from a New York City museum, Wonder Woman jumps into action.
But as Giganta makes her escape, the Amazon warrior realizes
there is more to the crime than meets the eye. Soon she discovers
that an old enemy plans to use the jar to plunge the world into war!
Can Wonder Woman stop Giganta, seal up the jar, and put an end
to the Pandora plot in time?

Designer: Kyle Grenz

Printed and bound in the USA

PO3074

TABLE OF CONTENTS

With countries in chaos and the world at war, Earth faced its darkest hour. To answer its cry for help, the Amazons on the secret island of Themyscira held a trial to find their strongest and bravest champion. From that contest one warrior—Princess Diana—triumphed over all and boldly entered the world of mortals. Now her mission is to conquer villainy, defend justice, and restore peace across the globe.

She is . . .

WONDER WOMAN™

CHAPTER 1

BIG TROUBLE

Diana Prince wove her way through a crowded New York City sidewalk. She was on her way to one of her favorite places in the city—a history museum. She knew it would be the perfect place to spend a few hours off from her duties as Wonder Woman. Not only that, but it would satisfy her longing for home. Looking at ancient artifacts reminded her of her birthplace, the island paradise of Themyscira.

WHEE·OO·WHEE·OO·WHEE·OO!

As Diana rounded a corner, police sirens rang out.

Uh-oh, she thought, *it sounds like the museum will have to wait.*

Diana ducked out of sight for a wardrobe change. In the blink of an eye, she returned to the sidewalk in the red-blue-and-gold uniform of Wonder Woman.

The Amazon Princess leaped into the sky and flew toward the sirens. To her surprise, they were coming from the very museum she had planned to visit.

On the street below, Wonder Woman spotted at least a dozen police cars with their lights flashing. Two dozen officers crouched behind them, aiming high-tech stun weapons at the museum's entrance.

Wonder Woman swooped down to ask the officer in charge what was going on.

CRASH!

The hero stopped short before she reached the officer. She spun around and looked up. To her surprise, a fifty-foot-tall, redheaded woman in a pink dress smashed through the museum's wall.

"Giganta!" Wonder Woman exclaimed.

The super-villain's incredible ability to increase her size—and her strength along with it—made her a very dangerous foe. But her exit from the museum puzzled the Amazon warrior.

At that size, Giganta isn't exactly good at sneaking around, Wonder Woman thought. *Why on earth would she . . .*

Then Wonder Woman spotted something small clutched in one of Giganta's massive hands. It looked like an ancient sealed jar with a tiny crack running down its side. Seeping from the crack were wisps of thick, black smoke.

I don't know what Giganta has stolen this time, Wonder Woman thought. *But it doesn't look good. Still, I can't risk fighting her in such a busy place. Too many people could get caught in the middle.*

"Giganta!" the Amazon warrior shouted. "Give back the jar, turn yourself in, and *no one* will get hurt!"

Giganta glanced down and flashed a wicked grin at Wonder Woman. A shiver ran down the hero's spine.

She looks like she wants to stomp me like a bug, thought the Amazon.

"That's a kind offer, Wonder Woman," Giganta answered in a booming voice. "But last night, I had a dream. In it a voice told me to do this." Then the villain pulled the lid off of the mysterious jar!

"It also told me that a whole *lot* of people *are* going to get hurt!" Giganta said as the mouth of the jar glowed with an eerie light.

ZAAP! ZAAP! ZAAP!

The police officers opened fire, peppering Giganta with bolts of energy from their stun weapons. The electricity would have knocked out a normal person, but it only tickled the towering villain. Meanwhile, the glow from the jar became brighter.

"Look out!" shouted Wonder Woman. But she was too late. The jar's glow quickly changed into black smoke that billowed toward them.

As the smoke covered Wonder Woman, she sensed something familiar.

This feels like some sort of magic, the hero thought. *Maybe even the kind used by the gods and goddesses of Olympus who gave me my powers!*

As the smoke began to clear, Wonder Woman looked in every direction. To her alarm, both Giganta and the ancient jar had vanished.

Where could she have gone so quickly? Wonder Woman thought. *Did the jar's magic whisk her away? Or is the mysterious voice she mentioned really at work here?*

The sound of footsteps behind her interrupted Wonder Woman's thoughts. She looked up just in time to see a police officer fire his weapon at her!

POW!

Before the Amazon could react, an expanding net flew from the weapon's barrel. In an instant, the net wrapped Wonder Woman up tightly.

That wasn't a misfire, the hero thought. *He fired at me on purpose!*

Wonder Woman gripped the net to tear it apart with her super-strength. But as she pulled at the netting, a powerful electrical charge ran through it.

TZZZZZZZZ!

Wonder Woman fell to her knees. As she struggled to her feet, the police opened fire with their energy blasters. In a blur of motion, Wonder Woman tore through the net and began deflecting energy bursts with her silver bracelets.

ZING! ZING! ZING!

Step by step, Wonder Woman drew closer to the officers. As she did, she noticed that her golden Lasso of Truth began glowing extra-bright!

Something about my lasso is fighting against the lingering smoke, she thought. *Then maybe it can . . .*

In a flash, Wonder Woman uncoiled her lasso and flung it at the nearest officers.

SWIPPP! SWIPPP! SWIPPP!

To her amazement, the officers fell to the ground unconscious the moment the golden rope touched them.

Moving quickly, the Amazon warrior used her lasso on the remaining officers. Soon, all of them were lying in the street, completely knocked out.

Wonder Woman coiled up her lasso and watched as several ambulances arrived on the scene. As emergency workers rushed to aid the officers, the hero jumped in to help.

I know Giganta is getting farther away with every passing minute, Wonder Woman thought. *But I need to see if the effects of the smoke will wear off before I go after her.*

But long after the smoke had cleared, the police officers were still asleep. And nothing Wonder Woman or the emergency workers did would wake them up!

CHAPTER 2

HISTORY LESSON

As the last ambulance took the remaining police officers to a nearby hospital, Wonder Woman raced across New York City. She headed straight for the Advanced Research Group Uniting Super-Humans headquarters. More commonly known as A.R.G.U.S., the government organization was responsible for helping super heroes and tracking down super-villains.

After racing through the front doors of A.R.G.U.S., Wonder Woman headed straight for the offices of agents Steve Trevor and Etta Candy. She was confident her friends could help her find Giganta.

Wonder Woman found Steve in Etta's office. The two agents were huddled around Etta's computer monitor watching news footage of Giganta's attack.

"Where could she have gone?" Wonder Woman asked.

"Maybe she just shrank down to normal size," said Steve, rubbing his chin thoughtfully. "If she did, she'd lose her strength, but could just blend into a crowd."

"It's definitely possible," Wonder Woman said. "If so, would we still be able to find her using your equipment, Etta?"

Etta began typing furiously on her computer keyboard. As her fingers danced across the keys, a bunch of screens lit up. They showed the streets around the museum from many different angles.

"These videos show ten blocks in every direction from the museum," Etta said. "Do you want me to speed up the footage?"

"Please," Wonder Woman answered.

Years ago, the gods and goddesses of Olympus had given Wonder Woman the powers of wisdom, beauty, strength, flight, and speed. They had also named her after Diana, the goddess of the hunt. And like her namesake, she had super-sharp eyesight.

As Etta ran the images at high speed, Wonder Woman easily spotted details that looked like blurs to Etta and Steve. But even with her great powers, she still found nothing. No sign of Giganta anywhere.

"Her sudden disappearance certainly makes a case for magic," said Etta. "Let's see if the museum has any useful information about that jar."

Steve used Etta's computer to look up the museum's database of artifacts, including items locked away in storage.

"Weird. Nothing in the museum's records shows anything that fits the jar's description," Steve said. "But we know Giganta *found* it there. Maybe we can run a picture of it through an image-identification program."

In a matter of moments, a clear image of the jar in Giganta's hands appeared on the screen. Steve's program didn't find any matches, but Wonder Woman's eyes narrowed as she got a better look at the ancient artifact.

"By Hera," she said in a voice barely louder than a whisper. "It can't be . . . it should be impossible."

"What is it?" asked Etta.

"The story is an old one," Wonder Woman said, turning to face her friends. "Once, long ago, the ancient gods trapped humanity's troubles in a jar. These included madness, disease, violence, fear, suffering, and—oddly enough—hope. Then the jar was brought to earth, where a woman named Pandora opened it. In doing so, she unleashed the jar's horrors on humankind."

"Wait," Steve interrupted, "Pandora? As in *Pandora's Box?* That story is real?"

"The term 'box' was a bad translation from ancient Greek. Some of the other details got changed a bit here and there over time too. But yes, the *jar* is real," Wonder Woman replied. "And only mortals can unleash the horrors within it. That's why it was placed on Themyscira, where my sisters, the Amazons, could keep it safe in a hidden vault."

"Wait just a minute. How could anyone steal the jar away from the Amazons?" asked Etta. "They're the greatest warriors in the world!"

"That's a *very* good question," Wonder Woman replied. "Giganta said a voice in a dream told her to go to the museum and use the jar. Whoever that was must have put it there. They also must have known only a mortal could open it."

The Amazon Princess sighed. "Oh, that poor girl."

"Poor girl?" replied Steve with a laugh. "Giganta?"

"Giganta is a victim here, Steve," Wonder Woman said. "She may be a criminal, but I've never seen her so happy about hurting people before. Someone is controlling her. It's up to me to save her."

"You always see the best in people, Diana," Etta said. "I hope your trust isn't misplaced."

"The jar isn't safe for anyone, no matter how strong they are. That's why even the Amazons keep their distance from the vault it's kept in on Themy . . ." Wonder Woman's voice trailed off.

The hero touched her hand to her tiara, activating a communicator that allowed her to contact home. After a moment, a worried look crossed her face.

"The Amazons aren't answering," Wonder Woman said. "I have to get to Themyscira right away!"

Dashing to a stairwell, Wonder Woman bounded up the steps five at a time. Steve and Etta struggled to keep up as they followed her to the roof.

"What about Giganta?" Etta asked as the three made their way to the rooftop's empty helipad. "We can't just let her get away."

"Keep looking for her. I doubt she has left the city," Wonder Woman replied. "I'll be back as soon as I can."

WHOOSH!

Strong winds suddenly kicked up all around them. The sound of a roaring engine cut through the air.

"I can have a helicopter here to take you to Themyscira in a few minutes," Steve shouted over the noise. "Just give me a moment to make—"

"Have you forgotten?" Wonder Woman said, stepping up into the air as if she were climbing an invisible ladder. "My ride's already here."

With a wave, Wonder Woman disappeared completely. Then the noise of the engine grew even louder before it finally trailed off into the distance.

"Invisible Jet," Etta teased. "Remember?"

* * *

Wonder Woman's jet rocketed across the Atlantic Ocean to the hidden island that was once her home. As she landed on a small airstrip, the hero grew even more worried. None of her Amazon sisters came out to meet her.

Leaving the plane behind, the Amazon Princess raced to the vault that once held the jar. The ground around its open door was littered with unconscious Amazon warriors. It looked as though they had knocked each other out in battle.

This is just like what happened at the museum, Wonder Woman realized. Then she paused as she sensed someone watching her from inside the vault.

"Whoever you are, show yourself!" Wonder Woman shouted as she walked inside. "I am Diana of Themyscira—"

"I know who you are," a familiar voice said from behind.

Wonder Woman turned to face the voice.

SLAPPPPPP! A hand in a metal glove smacked her. The blow sent her flying across the room and into a stone column. **CRACK!**

As the Amazon Princess struggled to her feet, she couldn't believe her eyes. Before her stood Philippus, one of Queen Hippolyta's most-trusted generals. She was also Diana's dear friend.

Wonder Woman choked back her shock. "Philippus? Where's my mother?"

"Wouldn't you like to know?" she answered, pointing a gleaming spear in Diana's direction. "I won't let you hurt her."

Hurt my mother? Wonder Woman was startled. *Philippus has been infected by the jar,* she realized. *And she thinks I'm her enemy!*

CHAPTER 3

HERO UNWELCOME

A chill ran down Wonder Woman's spine as Philippus glared at her.

What do I do? My powers give me the edge in sheer strength, the hero thought. *But can I really fight my own friend?*

Before Wonder Woman could decide, Philippus hurled her spear at her. Diana easily dodged the weapon, but Philippus knew her friend's fighting style well. The general struck with a sliding kick to Diana's legs. Wonder Woman tumbled to the ground.

"Oof!" Diana gasped.

Of course she can guess my every move, Wonder Woman realized. *She helped teach me how to fight when I was growing up, after all.*

Philippus ran across the room and pulled a huge sword and a heavy shield off the wall. Then she leaped into the air and swung the sword at her former student.

Wonder Woman rolled out of the way of the sword, but she couldn't avoid the shield. Philippus swung it down at Diana like an ax!

CLANNNNGG!

Sparks flew as Diana caught the shield between her bracelets. She stopped it just inches from her face.

I can't risk holding back any longer, Wonder Woman thought. *I have to find my mother and figure out where Giganta is taking the jar!*

Diana flew upward, lifting the shield high into the air—and Philippus with it! Then she dropped them both to the ground.

THUD!

Dazed by the impact, Philippus lost her grip on her sword. As she reached for it, Wonder Woman smashed it to bits with a powerful stomp of her foot!

Philippus raced to the other side of the room. The general dropped her shield and grabbed for a whip on the wall.

FWSSSSSH!!! Wonder Woman hurled her golden tiara.

THUNK! The tiara's razor-sharp edge cut the whip in two as it sank deep into the stone wall.

Philippus grabbed the tiara and pulled with all her might.

"You know, Diana, I've wanted this tiara ever since you took it away to play hero. Maybe today's the day I—*oof!*—take it back." But even Philippus's great strength couldn't remove the tiara from the wall.

As Philippus pulled harder, Wonder Woman uncoiled her golden lasso.

"I know this isn't how you truly feel, my friend," Diana said. "Pandora's Jar has clearly worked its evil magic on you. Give in to my lasso's power and take me to my mother so we can solve this problem together."

"I'm right here, daughter."

Wonder Woman turned to see her mother, Queen Hippolyta, at the entryway.

She looks weak, Diana thought. *The jar has taken its toll on her as well.*

Behind Hippolyta loomed a team of her own warriors.

"Stand down, Philippus," the queen ordered. "My guards will take my rebellious daughter prisoner."

Wonder Woman could tell the newcomers hadn't been close to the jar. There was no anger in their eyes.

"Mother! This isn't what it looks like," Diana exclaimed. "You're a victim of—"

"A victim of trusting my daughter, who has clearly gone mad!" said Hippolyta.

Now she's lying? thought Wonder Woman. *Another of the jar's curses is revealed.*

"She's stolen Pandora's Jar and attacked Philippus and her fellow Amazons!" the queen cried. "It's time to end this before she hurts anyone else!"

Hippolyta's guards charged at Wonder Woman with their swords flashing.

Diana picked up Philippus's shield and blocked the Amazons' swords. But Hippolyta's warriors were relentless, and they soon had Wonder Woman surrounded.

The soldiers grabbed Diana by the arms and legs, straining to hold her. Although Wonder Woman knew she could simply fly away, she didn't want to leave her mother under the jar's curse. Instead, she simply shrugged, sending the Amazons flying!

They'll do whatever it takes to keep my mother safe, Wonder Woman thought as the warriors regrouped. *But maybe there is still a way to reach my mother and stop them.*

As the warriors stepped closer, Wonder Woman kneeled and dropped her weapons. She even set her golden lasso on the floor.

"I know you don't believe me, but I'm on your side," the hero said in a calm voice. "I would rather surrender than hurt any of my sisters. You are only being loyal to my mother." Then Wonder Woman turned and gazed deep into her mother's eyes. "As loyal as *I'm* trying to be to her."

Philippus and the guards helped the Amazon Princess to her feet and began leading her away.

"Stop!" Hippolyta said in a strained voice. "Let her go!"

Philippus turned Wonder Woman around. Diana instantly saw in her mother's eyes that her plan had worked. Her willingness to give up instead of hurt her fellow Amazons, combined with the queen's love for her, had weakened the jar's curse. But it wouldn't work forever.

"Put the lasso on me, Diana," Hippolyta said, her voice weak. "I can't fight this much longer . . ."

The Amazons released Wonder Woman. She picked up her lasso and draped it over Hippolyta's shoulders. The queen's face immediately relaxed.

"Thank you, daughter," Hippolyta said. "We don't have much time. You know the jar was stolen, but you don't know why."

The queen paused to take a breath. She looked like she might faint at any moment.

"We are just a few short hours away from a once-in-ten-thousand-years alignment of the planets," Hippolyta explained. "If the jar is opened at just the right spot, the curses within will instantly spread across the world. After that, even closing it again won't restore the world to normal."

"I'm not going to let that happen," Wonder Woman said. "But mother, the jar was taken far away from here. Why are you and the Amazons still suffering its effects?"

"I had come to the vault because I knew the planetary alignment would make the jar a tempting target," Hippolyta said slowly. "And when *he* came for it, I fought him hard. In the course of our battle . . ." The queen started to lose consciousness. ". . . the jar was cracked. Until that leak is sealed, the victims will *stay* victims."

"Mother!" Diana shouted, hoping she could get one last answer before her mother collapsed. "Who took the jar?"

Hippolyta's eyes closed as she whispered one word to her daughter before slumping over. Diana's eyes grew wide.

Wonder Woman ordered her soldiers to take Hippolyta, Philippus, and the other injured warriors to the palace. One of the Amazons turned to Diana.

"Princess?" she asked. "Who did the queen say took the jar?"

"Ares," she said, "the God of War. And if I can't stop him in time, the jar will spread panic and violence everywhere. It will give him what he wants most—World War III!"

CHAPTER 4

BRIDGING THE GAP

Wonder Woman had mixed feelings as she boarded her Invisible Jet and took off for New York City. She hated leaving her mother behind, but she knew Queen Hippolyta would understand. Amazons had a deep sense of duty, and Diana's duty was to keep humanity safe.

And of the many threats to humanity, Ares—the God of War—was definitely one of the biggest.

Ares's sole purpose ran against everything the Amazons believed in. While they were masters of all forms of combat, war was never their goal. They believed in peace and wanted to turn their enemies into friends whenever possible.

Ares, on the other hand, thought war was the key to all advancement. It made humans develop new technology, from medicine to rocket ships. To him, war was not just the best way—it was the *only* way.

I must stop him, Wonder Woman thought as she flew her jet back to the United States. Flipping a switch on the control panel, she started a video call with Steve and Etta. She updated them on what she had learned.

"Our satellites haven't picked up any trace of Giganta while you've been away," said Steve. "She's definitely keeping a low profile."

"Ares hasn't shown up, either," said Etta.

"The God of War usually tries to stay hidden for as long as possible," Wonder Woman said with concern. "I'm guessing even Giganta doesn't know who she's working for."

"You're worried about her?" Etta asked over the video call.

"Ares never gives a second thought to the humans he meddles with, Etta," Diana explained. "His only concern is getting what he wants, when he wants it."

"I've checked on the planetary alignment your mother told you about," said Steve. "Our astronomical charts say it will happen when the sun sets here in New York City. But there's no way to know *exactly* where Ares will have Giganta open the jar. If only we could have placed a tracker on her."

"Wait a minute, Steve. That's it!" said Wonder Woman. "We *do* have a sort of tracker. The jar is leaking, which means everywhere Giganta goes, it's affecting the people nearby. See if you can track outbreaks of illness *and* violence, using the museum as a starting point!"

In a matter of moments, the A.R.G.U.S. computers gave Steve and Etta the answer they were looking for.

"Brilliant!" Steve exclaimed. "It's showing a straight line that points directly to . . . the middle of the East River?"

Diana used the wisdom the goddess Athena had given her to consider where Giganta could be going.

"I've got it," Wonder Woman said. "Ares must be steering Giganta to the abandoned military base on General's Island."

"You may be right," Etta replied. "The city plans to turn it into a park, but for now it's still loaded with abandoned buildings, military vehicles, and tunnels."

"Ares will think it's the perfect place to launch World War III," Wonder Woman said. "You and A.R.G.U.S. need to make sure nobody is on the island."

"We're on it," Steve replied.

"And Steve," Diana said, suddenly realizing Ares would want to cause a distraction to stall for time. "See if the police can clear the Brooklyn Bridge immediately."

By the time the Invisible Jet swooped toward the historic bridge, the police were almost done clearing it. Through her cockpit window, Wonder Woman saw a woman standing in the middle of the bridge's walkway carrying a large duffel bag.

"I had a feeling," Wonder Woman said out loud as she watched the woman refuse to leave the bridge with two officers. Suddenly, the woman broke away from them and began *growing*. Sure enough, it was Giganta.

The villain dove off the bridge. *SNAAAP!* Her large body ripped through the safety netting alongside the bridge like tissue paper. Then she tumbled into the water.

Moments later, Giganta's body grew out of the water. She now stood nearly two hundred feet above the river. Her duffel bag looked more like a necklace hanging around her neck.

That must be where she's keeping Pandora's Jar, Wonder Woman thought as she watched Giganta reach for the police officers. *I've got to get it away from her, but first I have to get her away from those officers!*

Wonder Woman swooped in with her Invisible Jet and struck Giganta in the back! The blow glanced off of the villain, but it was enough to send her reeling!

"Gahhh!" exclaimed Giganta, struggling to keep her balance.

SKREECH!

The super-villain's giant, flailing hand scraped against the unseen object. "Ow!" she shouted.

Looks like that worked, thought Wonder Woman as the officers ran to the end of the bridge. *Now I'd better land before Giganta takes down my jet without even knowing it's here!*

Activating the jet's pontoons, Wonder Woman made a water landing a safe distance from the villain. The cockpit popped open, and the hero flew out of the jet.

Tourists and police officers onshore cheered as Wonder Woman flew after Giganta. The villain had turned away from the bridge and was now wading toward General's Island.

The Amazon warrior closed the distance with incredible speed. She hoped to get her lasso around Giganta and shatter Ares's control over her. But as she threw the golden rope—*KABOOOOOOM!*—a bolt of energy came out of nowhere. The loop of her lasso missed its mark.

As Giganta stepped onto General's Island, Wonder Woman barely managed to stop herself from plunging into the water.

Overhead, the late-afternoon skies turned dark with storm clouds. Up ahead, the hero saw an armored figure with glowing red eyes hovering between her and the island.

"Hello, Amazon," echoed the figure's deep, gravelly voice across the water's surface. "It's only fitting that you're here to witness my greatest triumph. And there's nothing you can do to stop me."

Ares—the God of War—had revealed himself at last.

CHAPTER 5

THE ULTIMATE WEAPON

Wonder Woman knew Ares was her equal in brute strength. She needed to find another way to get past him to stop Giganta.

Hovering above the river, the Amazon smashed her bracelets together.

BOOOOOOM!

The shock wave sent a wall of water crashing into the angry god!

Taking advantage of the distraction, Wonder Woman flew past him to chase Giganta. But as she closed in, she felt a gloved hand grab one of her legs. *YANK!*

Ares flung Wonder Woman into one of the island's abandoned military buildings.

CRASH!

The rickety structure collapsed from the impact.

"I admire your determination, Princess," said Ares, floating over the rubble. "But my victory is certain. Giganta has the jar in place and, in just a matter of minutes, the setting sun will seal all of humankind's fate . . . forever!"

"Maybe so," said Wonder Woman as she heaved a heavy chunk of concrete at her enemy. "But I won't give up without a fight!"

"Fight?" Ares said as he deflected the concrete with a wave of his hand. "This barely qualifies as an argument! But if it's a fight you want . . . "

Ares gestured at several old military tanks sitting nearby. Sparks danced from his fingertips as he used his powers to load the tank cannons and turn them toward Wonder Woman. Then, with a snap of his fingers, they fired.

BOOM! BOOM! BOOM!

Using her bracelets, the Amazon warrior deflected every shell she couldn't dodge. Still, the hero was barely able to keep up with the attack. Even worse, the sun was getting very low in the sky.

Ares is stalling for time, thought Wonder Woman. *I need to find Giganta before the clock runs down!*

"Down . . . ," Diana whispered to herself. "That's it!" Then the Amazon dropped from the sky and vanished into the smoke of an exploding shell.

Ares floated to the ground. He expected to find Wonder Woman unconscious. Instead, all he found was rubble.

"Where is she?" the villain shouted. He leaped skyward to make sure the Amazon wasn't heading for Giganta.

Little did he know that Wonder Woman was no longer above ground at all. Instead, she raced through a series of tunnels hidden underneath the abandoned buildings.

"Thanks for the tip about these tunnels," said Diana, talking to Steve and Etta through her tiara's communicator. "Do you have a location for Giganta? I'm flying blind here."

"Our agents spotted her at Warriors' Hill, about a thousand feet north of you," said Steve. "There's some sort of energy field around her. It's keeping our weapons from having any effect!"

"It won't block me," Wonder Woman said with determination. "You and your team need to back off. This is going to come down to me and Giganta."

Moments later, the hero burst out of the ground inside the energy field. Just feet away, Giganta sat cross-legged. She cradled the jar in her lap, one hand on the lid. But the villain didn't respond to Wonder Woman's arrival. In fact, she didn't move an inch!

Pale and sweating, Giganta was clearly suffering from being near the jar. Its crack now leaked even more black smoke than it had at the museum.

She looks like she could pass out at any moment, thought Wonder Woman.

The Amazon Princess extended an open hand to Giganta. But the villain still didn't seem to know she was there.

"Giganta," Wonder Woman said in a calm, even voice, "give up the jar. I can help you. I know this wasn't your doing. I don't want to hurt you, but I'll take the jar by force if I must."

A look of pain crossed Giganta's face, and her whole body began to tremble.

Are my words breaking through to her? Wonder Woman thought.

Suddenly, Giganta swung a clenched fist—growing more enormous mid-punch.

WHAM!

Caught off guard by the blow, the hero tumbled across the hilltop.

"Time to admit defeat, Amazon," Ares said. He approached the energy bubble, which disappeared at his touch. Then he slowly walked up to Giganta.

The super-villain placed his armored hand on Giganta's trembling shoulder. "It is time, my servant. Open the jar and let the Age of War begin!"

As the last rays of daylight faded in the west, Giganta removed the lid. The full force of the jar's contents poured out of its mouth!

Diana launched herself at Ares, swinging wildly at him. He shrugged off every blow. Then he struck back, driving Wonder Woman to her knees with a powerful energy blast from his hand.

"Giganta! All isn't lost until the sun fully sets!" Wonder Woman yelled. The Amazon gasped as Ares continued firing on her.

"Remember, you're the *only* one who can stop this. Ares can't open it . . . I can't close it . . . it all comes down . . . to you, Giganta," Diana said.

"Pretty words, Princess," said Ares, towering over the hero. He prepared to deliver a final blow with both hands. But then, suddenly, Giganta pulled him into the air. She had grown one hundred feet tall!

SLAM!

Giganta dropped Ares and stomped him into the ground with her enormous foot.

BOOM!

But the energy needed for the attack was too much for Giganta. She collapsed and returned to her normal size. In the process, she dropped the jar. Its lid rolled to a stop at Wonder Woman's feet.

The hero handed the lid to Giganta, who was fading fast.

"Giganta," Wonder Woman begged, "you have to close the jar now!"

Moaning, Giganta closed the jar just as the sun fully set. But she was still sick, and getting worse.

The crack, Diana thought, *we have to close it before the harm that's been done can't be undone.*

HA! HA! HA! HA! HA!

Ares's laughter filled the air as he rose from Giganta's footprint. "You've stopped my plans, Amazon. But your mother, your fellow Amazons, and hundreds of humans are still suffering."

"There's still a chance," Wonder Woman said, handing her golden lasso to Giganta. "I'm trusting you to do the right thing."

Giganta took the lasso. As its power renewed her strength a bit, she wrapped the rope tightly around the jar.

At last, the crack closed completely. Instantly, Wonder Woman sensed that the victims of the jar's power were all beginning to recover.

"No!" Ares shouted as he teleported away. "You may have won this battle, Amazon. But *all* wars are mine to win in the end!"

A short time later, Steve and Etta raced up the hill with a group of A.R.G.U.S. medics. They gently placed Giganta on a stretcher and covered her with a blanket.

"Wonder Woman," Giganta called out, "why did you trust me with the lasso? It's your most powerful weapon."

The Amazon smiled. "Ares thinks humans are like him—hungry for power at any cost. But I knew better. Thanks for proving me right, Giganta."

As the A.R.G.U.S. team wheeled the villain away, Wonder Woman turned to Steve and Etta. "Besides, the lasso *isn't* my most powerful weapon."

Steve looked surprised. "It isn't? What is? Your tiara? The Invisible Jet?"

Rising into the air to take the jar back to Themyscira, Diana laughed.

"Think back to the Pandora story, Steve. In addition to people's troubles, the jar also held a powerful force for good. It's the most powerful weapon I, or *anyone,* can use to defeat the world's problems."

"What's that?" Steve asked.

"Hope."

Ares

BASE: Mount Olympus

SPECIES: Olympian God

OCCUPATION: God of War

HEIGHT: 6 feet 11 inches

WEIGHT: 495 pounds

EYES: Blue

HAIR: Blond

POWERS/ABILITIES: Immortality, unmatched strength, shape-shifting, teleportation, and indestructible armor. He is also a skilled military leader and strategist.

BIOGRAPHY: Although his father is Zeus, the King of the Gods, Ares has never fit in on Mount Olympus. From an early age, he vowed to conquer Earth and overtake the human race. As the God of War, he thrives on conflict and enjoys manipulating humans into fighting with one another. With the powers of teleportation, shape-shifting, and incredible strength, Ares excels at causing chaos and destruction across the globe. Thankfully, Earth has Wonder Woman on its side, born to stop Ares's threats of treachery and death.

- One trait Ares prizes the most is that the larger a conflict grows, the more his powers increase. The villain relishes this trait so much he once had a weapon built for him that could mimic it. The Annihilator was a self-propelled battlesuit that fed on human rage.

- The God of War has several children, each with their own evil powers. Phobos, the God of Fear, can turn any nightmare into a reality. Deimos, the God of Terror, has a beard of snakes with panic-causing venom. And Eris, the Goddess of Strife, can fill the hearts of her victims with hatred with just a bite of her Golden Apples of Discord.

- Ares might be Zeus's son, but the Amazon Princess counters him with powers she received from several goddesses. Demeter granted Wonder Woman strength and Aphrodite gave her beauty and a loving heart. In addition, Athena allowed her to talk to animals and Hermes granted her speed and flight. With these superpowers, Wonder Woman is Ares's most difficult foe.

BIOGRAPHIES

Author

Ivan Cohen has written comics, children's books, and TV shows featuring some of the world's most popular characters, including Teen Titans Go!, Batman, Spider-Man, Wonder Woman, Superman, the Justice League, and the Avengers. Ivan looks forward to reading this book to his wife and son in their home in New York City.

Illustrator

Cartoonist **Gregg Schigiel** is the creator/author/illustrator of the superhero/fairy tale mash-up *Pix* graphic novels and was a regular contributor to Spongebob Comics. Outside of work, Gregg bakes prize-winning cookies, enjoys comedy, and makes sure he drinks plenty of water. Learn more at greggschigiel.com.

GLOSSARY

alignment (uh-LYN-muhnt)—being in a straight line

artifact (AR-tuh-fakt)—an object used in the past that was made by people

database (DAY-tuh-bays)—a collection of organized information on a computer

humanity (hyoo-MAN-uh-tee)—all human beings

infected (in-FEK-tid)—filled with germs or viruses

pontoon (pon-TOON)—a float that helps a boat or vehicle stay above water

rebellious (ri-BEL-yuhss)—struggling against the people in charge

satellite (SAT-uh-lite)—a spacecraft used to send signals and information from one place to another

surrender (suh-REN-dur)—to give up or admit defeat

technology (tek-NOL-uh-jee)—the use of science to do practical things, such as designing complex machines

unconscious (uhn-KON-shuhss)—not awake; not able to see, feel, or think

DISCUSSION QUESTIONS

1. Ares uses his powers to control Giganta and help him carry out his plot to start World War III. Why do you think he needed her? What abilities does she have that he doesn't?

2. Wonder Woman feels sorry for Giganta and says she is a victim. Do you agree with her? Why or why not? Discuss your opinion.

3. Giganta turns on Ares and helps Wonder Woman in the end. Why do you think Giganta does so? How do her actions make you feel about the super-villain?

WRITING PROMPTS

1. Giganta has the power to increase her height, and her strength along with it. Imagine that you have the same power. Write a paragraph describing how you would use it for good. Then draw a picture of yourself in action!

2. Wonder Woman needs Etta Candy and Steve Trevor's help to foil Ares's plot. Write about a time when you needed someone's help. Explain why you couldn't have succeeded without that person.

3. At the end of the story, Ares gets away when he disappears. Where does he go, and what does he do next? Write a new chapter that explains Ares's next big plot against Wonder Woman.